This book is dedicated to my husband, the people of Ukraine and all people affected by conflict worldwide. Thank you Emma for all your help and support, and Bodhi for your inspiration.

When The Birds Went Travelling

Blue Tit's Visit To Ukraine

written and illustrated by
Wendy Kemp

Peace begins with a smile.

Hi, I'm Barnaby blue tit. I'd like to tell you my story. Like many others, my story begins with love. I was blessed with the deepest of loves when I met my wife, Bodhi. Our love was as perennial as the seasons and woven with magic and magnificence. She and I were together for many years and raised lots of beautiful chicks together.

Year after year, we would return to the same old bird box in our favourite garden. It sat on the edge of a garden studio above a Philadelphus bush which had the most magnificent smelling flowers. The kind people of our garden would clear out the box each year, ready for me to make a fresh, new nest for Bodhi's eggs.

Bodhi and I valued the simple things in life. Often, we would sit, drink tea and reminisce about the magical moments we had spent bringing up our chicks. About the nights we'd spent sitting, staring and waiting excitedly for our eggs to hatch. Oh how our eyes had ached from the long nights spent endlessly fetching food for our hungry young.

We would chuckle to ourselves when we recalled the night when I'd been so exhausted that I picked up a catkin to feed our chicks, thinking it was a caterpillar!

Bodhi was special. She had a heart of pure gold. She would often say to our chicks, "you can't always trust your mind but you can always trust your heart." She was the kindest bird I ever met. If she wasn't looking after our family, she was helping others. Each morning, she would wake up, shake her feathers and tell us that we had been blessed with another day; a day to do something meaningful. She made each day count.

As well as inspiring us all with her loving heart, Bodhi was beautifully creative. She loved nothing better than designing and arranging our nesting box each year with her ever-sophisticated styles. She had an eye for detail, forever adjusting the materials I brought back for our nest until they were just perfect. "Oh! Thank you, Darling. Can you just move it a little to the left?" she would say. Somehow, her adjustments made all the difference!

Us blue tits sit on our eggs for approximately two whole weeks. Putting all this love and care into creating our nest box each year gave us something beautiful to enjoy during our long waits. I suppose she was inspired by William Morris who said, "do not have anything which is neither useful nor beautiful in your home".

Bodhi's favourite flowers were sunflowers. When she laid her eggs, they were never in bloom, so each year I would buy some paint and decorate the outside of the box with these sunny yellow flowers. This daily reminder of the glorious sunshine would bring us cheer each time we returned to our nest. With warmth and brightness in our hearts, we would sing our song joyfully.

One spring, we had returned from our travels and were about to start a new family. This year's interior project was based on William Morris's trellis wallpaper designs. Excited and enamoured by the beauty of spring, I fluttered to gather bluebells and primroses from the countryside. Twig by twig, I wove a lattice from which to hang them. I carefully selected each one and placed them in a symmetrical pattern across the walls. I smiled to myself as Bodhi gently whispered, "Oh! Thank you, Darling. Can you just move it a little to the left?" Maybe I have a wonky eye when it comes to symmetry as she would say this every time!

"Whatever you build,

make it beautiful".

Bodhi Blue Tit

It took us several weeks but the end result looked fabulous! We had just finished the inside of the box and the nest was built to perfection. First a thick layer of moss, followed by lots of very fine, carefully selected twigs, topped off by the softest feathers and plenty of the finest fluff I could find. We laid together in total comfort and admired our beautiful home, breathing in the sweet scent of our floral arrangement. All that was left to do was for me to paint the outside with the sunflower design.

The next day, I flew home carrying buckets full of sunflower-yellow paint. Nothing could have prepared me for the sight that met my eyes as I peeped through the hole of our nesting box. A sight which tore my world apart, shattering my heart in an instant. Bodhi was dead.

As I battled through the overwhelming pain and horror of the realisation of my loss, I tried to figure out what had happened. Then, my eyes fell upon a great tit feather. Gertrude great tit had taken over our home. We knew that there was always a danger of this happening. It is not uncommon for us blue tits to be forced to abandon our boxes when we are invaded by great tits, seeking to lay their eggs. I know that Bodhi would have fought Gertrude bravely, determined to protect our home and raise our chicks. Sadly, this time, Gertrude was more powerful. Bodhi's body lay motionless; a single bluebell at her side. My heart wept. What was I to do?

Gertrude was out gathering food so I seized this one opportunity and ventured inside the box. Something was gleaming in the middle of the nest. Could it be? Bodhi had actually managed to lay her first egg! My heart pounding underneath my feathers, I hurried to gather it under my wing and flew, with haste and care, to my friendly neighbour, May.

May lived next door at Red House which, like ours, was clothed in flowers. She was a very elderly blue tit who no longer laid eggs of her own. She kindly took the egg from me and said she would sit on it and protect it with all her heart.

Lost in my grief, I decided to visit wise Zen Master Kingfisher. He always had good advice. Off I flew, a box of tissues tucked beneath my wing.

Kingfisher greeted me with his serene smile, nodding his head in an inviting way that brought me an instant sense of safety. We sat together in silence for a while. Just being in his loving presence brought me comfort. He listened wholeheartedly to my pain then waited in peaceful contemplation. I closed my eyes as he spoke, carried away, somewhere ethereal by his words.

"Your loss has caused you deep suffering, my friend," he began, "Take comfort, for her spirit lives on. Her presence is eternal and can be found all around you. She is the gentle breeze as it ripples through the leaves of your treetop perch. She is the shimmer of sunlight that twinkles like a spattering of diamonds in the stream as you quench your thirst. She is there in the endlessly shifting clouds above you, every time you take flight. She is everywhere. Returned to the universal whole from which she came. To which we all belong."

We sat in silence. I knew he could feel her presence. When he stopped talking, my thoughts and emotions returned, and with them the overriding sense of grief and hopelessness. His words had shown me a glimmer of possibility that one day I might just find peace in my heart and mind.

The Zen Master suggested I should do something to honour my wife. To discover my path, he said I must be still for a while. His words echoed in my head: "When you have let go of your thoughts, the answer will come."

That evening, I flew to sit in the topmost branches of a mighty oak. There I watched as the sun set, slowly silhouetting the trees in the distant forest as the sky turned crimson. It was beautiful. I sat, breathing deeply as the sun bathed the earth in majestic, golden light. For the first time in what seemed like forever, my mind was still and I felt calm. As I took in the magnificence of nature all around me, it suddenly came to me. Sunflowers! I would travel to a place where they grew in abundance! I would find my wife's favourite flowers and bring back some seeds to plant where she was buried.

Away I flew, heart brimming with purpose and hope. Off to a country called Ukraine, well known for its sunflowers. I held firmly to the largest suitcase I could carry. I would need plenty of room for the seeds that I wanted to bring back.

As I flew, I imagined the sunflower fields like an impressionist painting with azure blue skies and bright yellow swathes of colour. Colours just like the feathers of blue tits.

I flew past a myriad of landscapes before I arrived in Ukraine. As I began my descent, a strange feeling began to wash over me. My senses prickled into action, unsettling me. Something was not right. As I flew closer to the ground, I couldn't believe what lay before my eyes. Buildings and homes lay reduced to rubble. Explosions. Gunshots. Suffering on a horrific scale. What was happening? It made no sense to me. As I took a closer look, I could see that many humans had been killed or terribly injured. I fluttered to where a group of people sat and overheard them saying that they had no clean water or food. What horror had befallen this nation?

Dazed and confused, I knew in an instant that my plan had to change. I had to stay. I had to see what I could do to help all these people whose lives had been torn apart. The ear-shattering, agonising din of gunfire and bombs made my feathers shake uncontrollably. This was what war looked like.

As I ventured deeper into the carnage, I found a group of people who were helping others with lifesaving aid. They were giving out food, medicine and blankets. They were helping people to safety, repairing water stations and supporting the overrun hospitals. I saw others comforting those in their grief. What they were living through was worse than any nightmare imaginable, I could also see a beacon of light in the kindness and compassion of these helpers. Their sole purpose, in this moment, was to serve those who were suffering. These helpers were so brave, just like my Bodhi. I could see they were essential in this crisis and I felt helpless. What use was a tiny blue tit? Then it came to me. My song! I would give them the gift of my song, in hope that it might brighten their hearts and bring them some small comfort.

So, for the next four weeks, I sang with all that I had
to give. Flying each day from dawn to dusk, I
travelled from one town to the next, making sure that
I visited every street I could find. Anywhere that I saw
people, I'd hasten to share my song. While guns fired,
bombs fell, buildings crashed and crumbled to the
ground and people let out shouts of horror, I sang all
the louder, in hope that they could hear me. In my
heart, I knew the healing power of nature's beauty. I
wanted to protect them from the atrocities happening
all around. Sometimes I would notice a child glance
my way. I hoped my song would offer a little ray of
light in their darkened existence.

It was after five weeks of singing continuously that I lost my voice. All that singing had made my throat sore. I had nothing more to give.

Exhausted, I decided to journey back to my homeland. I needed to let myself recover and perhaps then I could come up with a plan for how to help the people of Ukraine.

As I travelled across the changing landscape, I spotted a field of sunflowers. I flew down and filled my suitcase. It gave me a chance to sit quietly for a while and breathe. The last few weeks had been so very difficult.

As I was collecting the seeds, I remembered Kingfisher telling me that I needed to do something meaningful. I had thought my purpose was in collecting these seeds to honour my wife. I had, by chance, ended up joining the efforts of The Red Cross. Bodhi would have been so proud of me. She always said everyone had the power to make a difference.

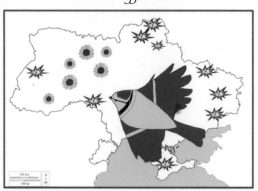

Upon returning back to the UK, my first port of call was to visit Zen Master Kingfisher. Kindly, he said I could stay with him for a while until I found a new home. We sat and drank tea and I told him tales of my travels. I told him all about the war and asked him why people fight and hurt each other. He told me, "while minds are filled with power, greed, fear and hatred, there will always be war. It is only when people work together and cooperate with kindness that the world will know peace." He explained that people must learn to release their anger and hatred if they are to transform their hearts and minds. "The world longs for this," he said softly.

After taking a slow, gentle sip of tea through his long beak, he turned to me and said, "you are much stronger than you were the last time that we met, dear Barnaby. You have made a brave choice in helping others. Compassion and tolerance are the embodiment of strength. Your heart has been filled by the kindness and care you have shown. It is truly as shining and golden as your wife's," he added, with a wink.

While minds are filled with power, greed, fear and hatred, there will always be war. It is only when people work together and cooperate with kindness that the world will know peace.

- Zen Master Kingfisher

*As evening drew in, I took the seeds that I had
collected to where Bodhi was buried. I sat and
reflected on the precious nature of life. How, in an
instant, everything you think you know can change.
On the impermanence of our homes, our relationships,
our bodies and our minds. Bodhi used to say,
"whatever you build, make it beautiful because you
can't hold on to it." I knew now that she didn't just
mean our home. She meant how we treat ourselves
and others too.*

*As I returned my mind to my task, I ruffled up the
soil and placed the seeds in a beautiful, circular sun
shape. To me, those tiny, precious seeds represented the
millions of refugees in Ukraine who had been forced
to leave their lives and homes and flee to unfamiliar
countries. I called the circular seed pattern my "seeds
of hope".*

As I held onto the last seed, I felt a warm glow building in my chest. It was a peaceful yet vast feeling of love that passed through my whole body. I could feel Bodhi's presence. Carefully, I positioned the last seed in the soil. I exhaled and closed my eyes, sensing that pure love was all around me. As I breathed, enjoying this moment, a familiar voice popped into my head:"Oh! Thank you, Darling. Can you just move it a little to the left?"I smiled.

I stayed there, present and simultaneously so very far away, for what felt like eternity.

"Dad?!"

A pretty voice shook me. I looked up and gazed into what seemed like a golden orb of light. Standing there before me was a perfect and radiant blue tit with beautiful feathers of such a vivid shade of yellow and blue. Colours that I had only seen on one other bird before. As I gazed upon our creation, my heart expanded like it had done the first time I'd seen Bodhi. She was perfect! We fluttered closer, feeling the joy of a field full of sunflowers as we breathed in each other's love.

Over the coming days, weeks and months, we began to build a home together. I named our daughter Bell after the bluebells Bodhi and I had collected together that spring when she was born.

Bell loved nothing more than hearing tales of her mother's loving heart and creative spirit. After hearing about the care and precision that went into our bird boxes, Bell was inspired and helped me to collect a stunning array of flowers. Together we weaved and arranged into our new family home.

Now, every morning, as we wake in our rose petal bed, we routinely smile, shake our feathers and ask, with a sense of adventure, "what can we do today that will benefit others?"

Oh, and just in case you were wondering, I still haven't got round to seeing someone about my wonky eye…

SEED OF HOPE

When The Birds Sang Louder written and illustrated by Wendy Kemp.

When The Birds Sang Louder is a touching and gentle reflection of COVID -19.
A keepsake to remember a time that changed the lives of every human on earth.
Weaved with underlying wisdom, this book will humble the hearts and minds
of any age.

A few independant Amazon reviews:
'Every and any age will benefit from this delightful story.'
'A book to cherish, to be read again and again'.
'A wonderful book full of positivity. A great way for children to read about
the times they lived through. A way for today's children to be able to tell the
next generation all about the pandemic! Fantastic illustrations. Beautiful words'.

Available on amazon www.amazon.co.uk/dp/B08NRXFRW

Printed in Great Britain
by Amazon